....

....

....

....

....

....

....

A
TREASURY
OF
Fairy
Tales

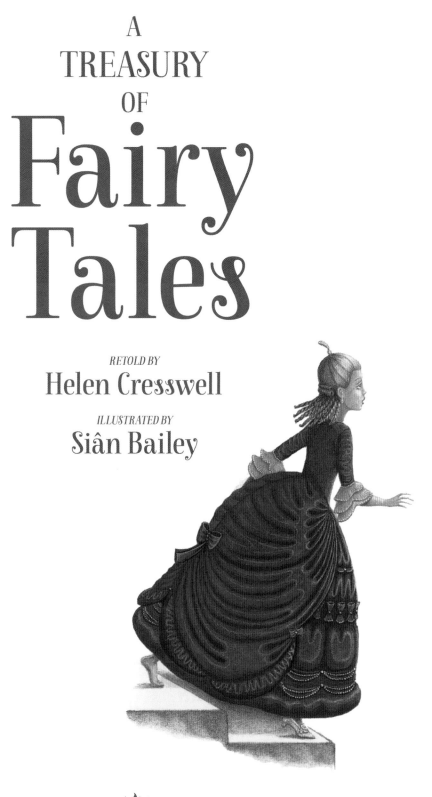

RETOLD BY
Helen Cresswell

ILLUSTRATED BY
Siân Bailey

HarperCollins *Children's Books*

For Little L with love
HC

For Felix, Oscar, Osian and Inigo with love
SB

First published in hardback in Great Britain as *Collins Treasury of Fairy Tales* by HarperCollins Publishers Ltd in 1997
This edition published by HarperCollins Children's Books in 2014

3 5 7 9 10 8 6 4 2

ISBN: 978-0-00-754651-0

HarperCollins Children's Books is a division of HarperCollins Publishers Ltd.

Text copyright © Helen Cresswell 1971
Illustrations copyright © Siân Bailey 1997

Visit our website at: www.harpercollins.co.uk

Printed in China

Contents

Beauty and the Beast

There was a once a wealthy merchant who had lost his wife but had three sons and three daughters. The sons were fine young men and the three girls were all beautiful, but the youngest in particular was so lovely that right from being a little child she had been called 'Beauty'. She was as kind and wise as she was beautiful, and her elder sisters, who were vain and proud, were both jealous of her.

Then the merchant lost his fortune and all he had left was a cottage in the country with a few acres of land around it. He called his children together and told them what had happened.

"We must go and live in the cottage," he told them, "and make our living as honestly as we may, and try to be happy."

The two elder daughters laughed the idea to scorn.

"Live in the country?" cried they. "In a cottage? That is hardly the life for us! We shall get married."

But now that they had no fortune, nobody wanted to marry them, and so they were forced to go to the country after all. The family settled in the cottage and the merchant and his sons set to work to dig and till the land. Beauty herself rose at four every morning and spent the whole day cleaning and cooking and looking after her hens. The only ones who were bored were the two sisters, who got up late and then spent the whole day idling and talking about the old days when they had been rich and gone to fine balls every night of the week.

After a year or so the merchant had a letter to tell him that a ship on which he had valuable cargo had come safely into port. Overjoyed, he prepared himself for the journey to go and collect the money. Before he left, he called his three daughters and asked each of them what she would like him to bring back as a present. The two elder sisters greedily prepared such long lists of gowns and hats and mantles that their poor father secretly wondered if there would be any money left once he had bought them all.

When it came to Beauty's turn to choose, she did not wish to ask for anything at all, but knew her sisters would think her priggish if she asked for nothing, so she replied, "I wish I could have a rose – just a single rose. There are none in our garden here in the country, and I long to see and smell one again."

The father set off with high hopes, but when he reached the port he found that he still owed so much money that when he had paid it all, there was nothing left. So he turned back home no richer than he had started, and was sad at heart to think that he could not afford to buy the presents he had promised his children.

When he was only thirty miles from home, and riding through a great forest, it began to snow. The flakes whirled so thickly that he could see only a few yards before him, and soon he had taken a wrong turning and was quite lost. It was growing dark, and far off he heard the wolves howl. He stumbled, and fell into the snow, and lay there for a minute in despair. Then he began to pull himself to his feet, and lifted his head and saw golden bands of light shining through the curtain of snow. He made towards them and soon he saw that the light shone from hundreds of windows of a great castle, and thankfully he led the horse within the stone walls of the courtyard. There the door of a stable stood open, and he saw a manger filled with corn and hay. The tired horse trotted gratefully inside and was soon well fed and ready for the night.

The merchant himself then went to the house, but there was not a sign of life. All was brilliantly lit and warm, but absolutely silent. He pushed the door and went in and found himself in a dining hall where a fire blazed and a table stood set ready for one person. He went to the fire and warmed himself and cast longing looks towards the fine supper, but though he waited and waited, nobody came. By eleven o'clock he was so ravenously hungry that he said to himself, "Surely, whoever is master here will pardon me if I take some food?"

And he went and took some chicken and then some wine and some fruit and soon began to feel better. He went out and began to explore the palace and soon found himself in a rich apartment set out ready as if for a guest. Here he lay on the bed and was soon asleep.

When he awoke next morning the first thing he saw was a new suit of clothes laid where his own wet and muddy things had been the night before.

"This palace must surely belong to a good fairy," thought he. He dressed and went down to find a fire blazing and the table set with hot toast and steaming chocolate.

When he had eaten the merchant went out to his horse and saw that the snow had all gone and the sun was shining over green lawns and curving fountains and great banks of beautiful roses. At the sight of the flowers he suddenly remembered Beauty's parting wish, and as he went under an archway, reached up and snapped off a single red rose.

As he did so there came a terrible roar and the merchant turned to find himself face to face with a beast so horrible that he almost fainted right away with terror.

"So this is your gratitude!" snarled the Beast. "I have saved your life by taking you into my castle, and you repay me by robbing me of my roses, that I love more than anything else in the world! And you shall die for it!"

The merchant threw himself on his knees.

"Pardon me, my lord! I meant no harm! I was only plucking a single rose to take to one of my daughters who had asked me to bring her one!"

"I am not called 'My Lord', but 'The Beast,'" snarled the terrible creature then. "And whether you meant to take one rose or a thousand makes not a whit of difference. But you say you have daughters at home. Very well. If one of them will come willingly here, and give her life in your place, then you may go free. But if none of them will do this, you must give me your promise that you will return here yourself three months from this day."

The merchant had no intention of letting one of his daughters die instead of himself, but he thought, "This gives me at least a chance to go and see them for the last time, and say my farewells," and so he agreed, and gave his promise. Then the Beast told him to go back to his room in the castle where he would find an empty chest.

"Fill it with as much treasure as you can carry," said the Beast. "There is no need for you to go away empty handed."

With this he disappeared. And so the merchant rode home laden with riches after all, though his heart was sadly laden too.

When he reached home his family rushed to welcome him and the two elder sisters clamoured for their gifts. The merchant shook his head and took the rose and gave it to Beauty, saying, "Take your rose, my Beauty, and enjoy it while you may, for it has cost your poor father very dear!"

Then he told them the whole story, and when he had finished the two elder sisters cried, "There! See now what you have done, Beauty, with your childish requests!"

The three brothers cried, "Only tell us where this monster lives, and we will go and kill him!"

"He would kill *you*," replied the merchant. "No, there is nothing else for it. I must die."

But when the three months were up, Beauty went with her father to the Beast's castle determined that she would take his place. No one could stop her, and as the pair left the cottage the brothers wept and the two sisters cried tears they had made by rubbing their eyes with an onion.

The merchant's horse guided the pair to the Beast's palace of his own accord, and they found it brightly lit as before.

A fine meal was set out for two people and they sat to their supper, though they were too sad to be hungry and only ate each to please the other. As they rose from the table there was a terrible growling, and there stood the Beast himself before them. He asked Beauty whether she had come readily, of her own free will, to take her father's place, and when she answered "Yes", he said to her, "You are a good girl, and I am obliged to you."

Then he told the merchant that he might stay in the palace for the night, but that next morning he was to go and never return again.

When Beauty had parted from her father next morning, she threw herself down and wept bitterly. When she was calmer she sat up and looked about her and began to wonder what strange kind of place this was. She walked through the lovely gardens and then explored the palace itself. The more she saw, the more she had the strange feeling that it had all been planned specially for herself, and no one else. Even her favourite books stood upon the shelves and the rooms were furnished with the colours she loved best. She took down one of the books, and read in gold letters,

"Desire. Command. You are Lady and Mistress here."

"Alas!" sighed Beauty. "All I desire is to see my poor father and know how he is."

She laid down the book and looked up, straight into a large mirror that hung on the wall opposite. There, in the glass, she saw the cottage and her father entering it, his face full of grief. Then her sisters ran out to greet him, and as she watched the picture faded and they were gone. But now her heart was lighter, for she thought, "The Beast is perhaps not so fierce as he seems. Surely if he were, he would not have done such a thing to make me happy?"

At supper that evening the Beast appeared again and though Beauty trembled with terror she forced herself to look at him and answer his questions.

"Beauty," growled the monster, "are you willing to let me look at you while you sup?"

"You are master here," replied Beauty.

"No!" replied the Beast. "You alone are mistress here. If you bid me go away, I shall go. And it would be no great surprise if you did so. Tell me, am I not the ugliest thing you ever set eyes on?"

"You *are* ugly" agreed Beauty, not wishing to tell a lie. "But I begin to think that you are very kind. And when I think how good you are at heart, then you no longer seem quite so ugly to me."

The Beast seemed pleased by her words and sat quite still and watched while she finished her supper. Then, quite without warning, he said,

"Beauty, will you be my wife?"

She was so shocked by the question that at first she could find no words to answer, but replied simply at last, "No, Beast."

At this he let out a shriek of pain so terrible that the whole palace shook and Beauty thought her last hour had come. But the Beast, once he had recovered, only said gently, "Goodnight, then, Beauty," and went to the door, with a last wistful look at her before he went. Beauty, seeing his large, reproachful eyes, was filled with pity.

"Poor Beast," she thought. "To be so kind of heart and yet to be so ugly."

Three months passed by, and each day Beauty amused herself in the palace and gardens, and each evening the Beast came to visit her. As the days passed, she became used to his ugliness and even began to look forward to seeing him at night. There was only one thing she dreaded, and that was the time when, before he left her, he would ask her the same question, night after night.

"Beauty, will you marry me?"

And each night she was forced to answer "No," and to see his pain and sadness. One evening she said to him, "Beast, I only wish that I could marry you, but I cannot bring myself to pretend what I do not feel. I shall always be your friend – can you not be content with that?"

"I suppose I must," replied the Beast. "And I cannot blame you, for I know how horribly ugly I am. But I love you more than life itself – will you at least promise me that you will never leave me?"

Now that very day Beauty had looked into the magic looking glass and seen there pictures of her father who had become ill with grief at losing her.

"I would willingly promise never to leave you altogether!" she cried. "But I long so much to see my poor father again that I fear both he and I will die of grief if I cannot visit him!"

"I would rather die myself than make you unhappy," said the Beast. "But if I send you home, then you will never come back, and then your poor Beast will die of grief!"

"Oh no!" cried Beauty, weeping. "I love you too much now to wish to cause your death. If you let me go to my father, I promise I shall return in eight days."

"You shall be there in the morning," the Beast told her. "And when you wish to return, lay your ring on the table before you go to bed. And remember your promise, Beauty – eight days. Goodbye!"

The Beast gave his usual great sigh and left her for the night, and when he had gone Beauty went to bed and wept into her pillow, grieved that she should have hurt him. When she awoke next day she was in her father's house, and the whole household was amazed at her marvellous reappearance. Her father was beside himself with joy, and begged Beauty to hurry and dress and come downstairs so that they would have the whole long day together.

Then Beauty realised that she had no clothes to put on, but the maid came and told her that she had just found a chest in the next room, and that it was filled with beautiful and costly gowns. Beauty's eyes filled with tears as she remembered the poor, ugly Beast and saw how well and faithfully he looked after her.

Beauty's father was soon well again, and one day her sisters came visiting with their husbands. They were filled with spite and envy when they saw Beauty looking so happy, lovelier than ever and dressed like a princess. When they learned of the promise Beauty had made to the Beast, they began to plot against her.

"We will persuade her to overstay her visit," said the eldest. "Then the Beast will be so enraged that he will devour her, and we shall be rid of her forever!"

"Perfect!" cried the other. "We will pretend to be very fond of her, and beg her to stay longer with us, and she is so soft-hearted that she is bound to give in!"

And so it happened. On the eighth day, when Beauty was preparing to leave, her sisters made such a show of grief and wept so loudly and implored her so desperately to stay longer with them, that Beauty was quite overwhelmed.

"I had not known that they loved me so dearly," she thought. "And surely there is no great harm in staying just a little longer to make them happy?"

And so she gave in and stayed, and the wicked sisters gloated secretly and were certain that soon she would pay for it with her life.

But on the tenth night of her visit, Beauty had a dream. She dreamed that she saw the Beast lying weak and dying in the grass, and reproaching her for breaking her promise to him. Beauty woke with a start and began to weep.

"Poor Beast!" she cried. "How could I be so wicked and thoughtless! Ugly as he is, he has shown me nothing but gentleness and kindness, and this is how I repay him!" She took off her ring, placed it on the table beside the bed, and went to sleep again. When she awoke, she was back in her room at the Beast's palace.

She spent the day happily enough and towards evening went and dressed in her most beautiful gown to give the Beast pleasure, and eagerly went down to supper to meet him.

The clock struck nine, but the Beast did not appear. Beauty knew at once that something was amiss, and began to run about the empty palace, vainly calling his name. Then she ran out into the gardens, remembering that in her dream she had seen the Beast lying in the grass near the brook. And it was there that she found him, lying with his eyes closed, looking as though he were already dead.

Beauty ran and flung herself to her knees beside him. She lifted his great head and cradled it in her lap, stroking it and weeping and crying, "Oh Beast, Beast, my dear Beast, what have I done to you?"

She thought she saw his eyelids flicker, and ran straightway to the brook for water to set her handkerchief. Then she bathed his forehead, murmuring his name as she did so, and at last the Beast's eyes opened and he looked up at her.

"You forgot your promise," he said faintly. "But now that I have seen you once more, I shall die happy, looking on your beloved face."

"No, dear Beast, you shan't die," cried Beauty. "You must live and become my husband. I know now that I love you truly, and want nothing more than to become your wife and make you happy. You must live, Beast, for my sake!"

No sooner had she spoken these words than the whole palace was suddenly lit from within and beautiful music began to play. She turned her head to look, and when she looked back to the place where the Beast had been lying an instant before, there knelt a young Prince, bright as the day.

"Where is my Beast?" cried Beauty.

"I am he," came the reply. "Thanks to you, dear Beauty, I am a Beast no more. I was doomed by a wicked fairy to take the shape of a horrible beast until of her own free will someone should come to love me and consent to marry me."

And so Beauty and her Prince went together into the lighted palace where they found her father, and were married in his presence that very day.

As for the wicked sisters, they were turned into stone statues and forced to stand forever, one each side of the palace door, and watch their sister living happily with her Prince for the rest of her days.

Cinderella

There was once a man whose first wife had died, and so he married again. He did not pick so well the second time. His new wife was spiteful and bad-tempered and to make matters worse, she had two daughters who both took after her.

This man already had a daughter, and she was kind and gentle and beautiful. So the stepmother and her daughters were thoroughly jealous of her, and soon set about making her life as miserable as they could.

They gave her all the dirty work in the house. She scrubbed and scoured and dusted all day long while her new sisters lay polishing their nails or prinking themselves in the glass. They wore jewels and silks and satins while their poor sister had only a few rags to her back. They slept on soft feather mattresses, deep and warm, while she shivered on straw in the draughty attic.

And she patiently worked and shivered and half-starved without saying a single word of complaint to her father.

At the end of the day when all the work was done, she would sit huddled among the cinders in the chimney corner of the kitchen, trying to keep warm. Even this did not make the ugly sisters sorry. Instead, they laughed, and gave her the nickname of Cinderella.

One day, the king of all the land gave a great ball for his son, the prince. The stepmother and her daughters were invited, and were soon busily planning what they would wear and how they would dress their hair.

While the two ugly sisters posed before the glasses, trying out sashes and twirling their hair into ringlets, Cinderella was sent rushing hither and thither to fetch and carry, to sew and press, so that everything would be ready on the night of the ball. Instead of being grateful for her help, the two sisters mocked her.

"How would you like to go to the ball, Cinderella?" they asked.

"Oh, I would!" she cried wistfully. "But people would only laugh. Look at me, in my old rags!"

"Laugh? I should think they would!" cried the two sisters. "A fine sight *you* would be at the king's ball!"

On the great day Cinderella worked harder than ever in her life before, trying her hardest to send her sisters off to the ball looking their very best. And when the last bow was tied and the last ringlet curled, they *did* look their very best – though even that was not saying very much.

Off they went with a proud flurry of rustling skirts, out to the waiting coach, with not so much as a wave of the hand to Cinderella, let alone a thank you. When the sound of the carriage wheels had died away and she was alone at last in the great, empty house, Cinderella crept back to her usual place by the hearth, and began to cry.

After a while she heard a knocking at the door, and drying her eyes, went to answer. In stepped a little old woman who looked like a beggar in her tattered cloak.

"Why are you crying, child?" asked she.

"Because… because…" Cinderella did not like to say why she was crying.

"You need not tell me," said the old lady surprisingly. "I know quite well why you are crying. It is because you want to go to the ball."

Cinderella stared at her.

"I am your godmother," explained the other then. "Your fairy godmother. And now, child, there's work to be done. Go out into the garden and fetch a pumpkin, quick!"

Cinderella was out in the garden searching for a pumpkin before she had even time to think. When she brought it back, her godmother rapped it smartly with a long black stick – or was it a wand? – and there in a trice stood a golden carriage! It winked and glittered and shone bright as the sun itself.

"Two mice!" ordered the godmother, without a blink.

Cinderella opened the pantry door and as two mice came scampering out
– poof! A wave of the magic wand and they were high-
stepping horses with flowing manes and rearing heads.

"What about a coachman?" murmured the godmother.
"Run and fetch the rat-trap, will you?"

Cinderella did not wait to be asked twice. Off she ran to
fetch it, and next minute there stood a stout coachman with brass buttons
and a large three-cornered hat.

"If you look behind the watering can beside the well," went on the
godmother, without so much as the twitch of an eyebrow, "you will find
six lizards. We could do with them, I think."

Sure enough, there were the six lizards exactly where she had said, and
a flick of that busy wand transformed them instantly into six tall footmen
with dashing liveries.

"Well!" exclaimed the fairy godmother then. "That carriage could take
a *queen* to the ball. Do you like it?"

"Oh, it's beautiful!" cried Cinderella. "But godmother, I still can't go to
the ball!"

"And why not?"

"My dress! Look at me! Whoever saw a sight like this at a king's ball?"

"That is easy enough," replied the old lady. "Stand still a moment, child,
and shut your eyes."

Cinderella stood quite still, her eyes tight shut. There was a slow, cool
rustling, a breath of scented air and a soft silken brushing and then
"Open!" commanded that thin, high voice.

Cinderella opened her eyes.

"Oh!" she gasped. It was all she could say. "Oh!"

About her, billowed the most beautiful dress she had ever seen, sky blue
and stitched with pearls, threaded with silver. And there, beneath the hem
of her skirt, glittered a pair of shining crystal shoes.

"Glass slippers!" gasped Cinderella.

"Off you go now, child," said her godmother briskly. "Off to the ball
and enjoy yourself!"

Cinderella gathered up her shimmering skirts and stepped into the golden coach. The footmen bowed. The coachman lifted his whip.

"Wait!" cried the godmother.

Cinderella put her head out of the carriage window.

"Home by twelve sharp! Do you hear? Not a minute later!"

"I shall be back," promised Cinderella.

"Listen for the clock," warned her godmother. "Not a single moment after the last stroke of twelve. If you're even a second late –"

"What?" cried Cinderella in alarm. "What will happen, godmother?"

The old lady waved her arms.

"Poof! Gone! Coach to pumpkin, horses to mice, coachman to rat – poof! Gone! All of it!"

"I'll remember," cried Cinderella. "I promise. The last stroke of twelve! Goodbye, godmother! And thank you!"

She had a last glimpse of her godmother's shabby figure and then the coach was rolling on its way. She, Cinderella, was off to a king's ball!

When at last the golden coach reached the palace gates the news was quickly spread about that a great lady, certainly a princess, had arrived at the gates. Servants and flunkeys ran to bow and open doors and make a way for Cinderella through the crowds of staring guests. For she was so beautiful that all the people stood quite still to watch her as she passed, and even the music faded as the fiddlers laid down their bows in wonder.

The king's son himself watched her walk among the whispering guests. He went to greet her, and was in love before he had even reached her side. He led her on to the floor to dance and the fiddlers picked up their bows again and began to play.

All the evening long the two of them danced together. The prince could not bear to leave Cinderella's side for even a moment. The other guests were filled with envy and curiosity, and the two ugly sisters were angriest of all. Not a single dance had either of them had with the prince all night.

"Whoever can she be?" they cried, craning to peer at her each time she whirled by. Not for a single minute did they suspect that the beautiful stranger was none other than their sister, Cinderella.

Cinderella herself was so happy that she forgot all about the time. The great ballroom clock was already beginning to chime the hour for midnight when she suddenly remembered her godmother's warning and her own promise to be home by twelve.

"O!" she cried. "I'm late! The time!"

Before the astonished prince could collect his wits she had darted off and was out of the ballroom and running down the great marble staircase to her waiting coach.

Six… seven… eight… the bell was chiming.

The coach clattered away out of the palace courtyard. At the top of the staircase the prince stood looking left and right for a sign of his vanished

25

partner. He set the servants to search and they ran all through the palace, but in vain. She had gone. Only there, lying half way down the stairs, was a tiny glass slipper – Cinderella's. Sadly the prince picked it up and wandered away. He did not dance again that night.

Meanwhile, Cinderella was hardly out of the palace gates when – poof! The spell was broken. All in a moment she found herself out on the empty road and of the shining coach, the footmen and the coachman, there was not a trace. From the corner of her eye she saw running over the road a thin dark shape, that might have been a lizard. And that was all. Clutching her thin rags about her she set off home. Safely there, she climbed up to her cold attic and fell asleep, dreaming of the ball and the handsome prince.

The prince himself did not sleep at all that night. He paced up and down his room, clasping the glass slipper.

"I must find her," he said out loud. "And when I have found her, I shall marry her, and make her my princess."

Next day the king called his royal herald.

"Take this glass slipper," he commanded, "and search the length and breadth of my kingdom to find the young lady whose foot it fits. When you have found her, bring her to me. For she is the one the prince will marry."

Soon the news was spread about the town and the king's herald was going from door to door reading his proclamation and trying the slipper on one foot after another. He had not known there were so many feet in the world. Then at last he came to the house where the two ugly sisters had been eagerly awaiting his visit, their hair tightly curled and their legs trembling with excitement. One of them, for sure, would fit her foot into the glass slipper and become the prince's bride.

At last they heard a loud knocking on the door, and the notes of the herald's trumpet.

"Quick!" hissed their mother. "Sit down and look as if you weren't expecting him. And make sure one of you gets that slipper on!"

With that, she sent a servant to open the door, and next minute they were all curtseying to the king's messenger.

The two ugly sisters tried with all their might and main to fit their great feet into that dainty slipper. They squeezed and tugged and twisted and muttered and groaned, but all in vain. At last, sulky and red-faced, they gave up the attempt, trying hard not to catch their mother's eye.

"Is there no other young lady in the house?" asked the herald then. "I have orders to miss not a single one, whoever she is."

"No!" cried the three ladies together. "There's no one else!"

But just then, Cinderella herself came into the room, carrying a pail. The ugly sisters tried to shoo her from the room, but the herald bowed politely to her and offered her a seat while she tried the slipper.

Cinderella sat down, held out her foot, – and slid it smoothly into the tiny glass slipper!

"It fits!" cried the ugly sisters together. "It can't! It's a trick!"

Cinderella smiled, and taking from her pocket the other slipper, placed it on her other foot. And at that moment, her fairy godmother appeared and with a touch of her magic wand transformed Cinderella's rags into a snow-white bridal gown.

Only then did the others recognise her as the beautiful stranger at the ball. The ugly sisters and their unkind mother hurried off, afraid of what might happen to them when their wickedness was discovered.

But Cinderella forgave them willingly, and was driven off in the king's own coach to meet her prince again. And they were married that very same day, and lived happily ever after.

Dick Whittington

Once upon a time, long long ago, a little orphan boy named Dick Whittington came from the country up to the great city of London.

"The streets of London are paved with gold," he had heard the villagers say as they told tales under the chestnuts on summer evenings, or by the fireside in winter. And so Dick set out to see for himself. He was ten years old, alone in the world, and determined to make his fortune.

He was hungry and footsore when he came to London after days of travelling through the countryside, begging food and sleeping in barns and under hedges. But when he saw the domes and spires ahead of him against the sky, he hurried his pace, eager for a glimpse of those marvellous golden streets.

But as he entered the city at last, the stones beneath his feet were grey – as grey as ever they had been in any other town he had known. On and on he walked, hoping with every mile that he would round a sudden corner and see before him a street of purest gold, where he could stoop and gather up the golden cobbles and cram his pockets with them and be rich for the rest of his life.

But the people of London did not *look* rich — they did not even look so well and happy as the villagers at home. They walked in tatters with bent shoulders, though now and then a rich coach would go rolling by, with liveried footmen hanging on behind. Dick slept that night huddled in a doorway, and next morning, wandering through the narrow streets in a thin drizzle of rain, he suddenly lost heart, and said to himself,

"I have come on a wild goose chase. I shall go back home, to my own village, and work in the fields and be as happy as I can."

Sad at heart, he began to retrace his footsteps, and soon was outside the city and walking in the open country back towards home. He sat down propped against a milestone, and opened his bundle to find his last piece of cheese. As he sat there, the sound of bells was wafted over the fields from the city churches. They rang sweet and clear, and as Dick listened, he seemed to hear what they were saying:

Turn again Whitting-ton
Thou worthy cit-izen
Lord Mayor of Lon-don!

He leapt to his feet and stood with ears cocked. Again the peals came on a light wind, and as Dick stared back towards the city the sun suddenly struck through the clouds and shone on the wet roofs, turning them to gold.

Turn again Whitting-ton
Thou worthy cit-izen
Lord Mayor of Lon-don!

"And so I will!" cried Dick. And he picked up his knapsack and turned his face again towards the city.

That night he slept on a doorstep again, but this time he was discovered at dawn by a red-faced Cook, who opened the door and stirred him with her foot.

"You'll make a fine scullion!" cried she. "Lazy layabout – asleep at this hour! Five o'clock in the morning, and still fast asleep! You'd best come in and have breakfast and get started working!"

Dick followed her inside, scarcely believing his luck. He had not known that the household was looking for a scullion, but now, it seemed, he had the job, and was glad of it. He was given a room up in the garret, paid a penny a week and given a new suit of clothes. He worked from morning till night in the kitchen, and Cook scolded him if he did not wash behind his ears and keep his nails clean. But if he did, she would cut him a big slice of jam pie, so Dick's face was usually red and shining with soap and water.

This house belonged to a rich merchant named Fitzwarren, who had a little girl of nine years old called Alice. One day, she came down to the kitchen wearing a blue silk dress and a coral necklace. She stared at Dick, who was shelling peas in a corner.

"Are you the raggedy boy who came from the country?" she asked. "You look quite clean to me."

"That's because Cook chases me with her broom if I'm dirty," replied Dick. "Besides, I'm used to being clean now, and quite like it."

Alice drew up a stool nearby and asked Dick questions about his old life in the country and how he had come to London. So Dick told her about how he had set back home when he had found that the streets of London were not paved with gold after all, and how he had heard the bells calling him back:

Turn again Whitting-ton
Thou worthy cit-izen
Lord Mayor of Lon-don!

"And perhaps I *shall* be Lord Mayor, one day," he said, because even if he did sleep in a garret and spend the day scouring dishes and sweeping floors, he still had his dreams.

Alice laughed and spread out her silken skirts and said, "Well, you are quite a clean boy now, and sometimes I may come down to the kitchen and talk to you. But you are only a scullion and I am a lady, so you may not smile at me unless I smile at you first."

After that, Alice used to come down and talk to Dick sometimes, and he was well pleased with his life, except for one thing. The garret where he slept was overrun by rats, that scampered all over his bed when he was asleep. So he saved his wages and spent threepence on the biggest cat he could find. Soon all the rats had disappeared, and the cat would purr on Dick's bed at night instead, and keep his feet warm.

In those days, when merchants sent a ship to trade with Africa, everyone who worked for them could send in the ship a bale of goods, whatever he liked. This was called a 'Venture' or 'Adventure'. One day, Fitzwarren said to Dick, "Next week my new ship sails for Africa. What will you send as a Venture?"

"I have nothing," replied Dick. "Nothing but my cat, that is."

"Then you had better send the cat," said the merchant. "Every single one of us must send a Venture, or it will mean bad luck for the new ship."

So when the ship sailed, Dick's cat went with it, and it came to port in Africa, where the rich Sultan was eager to see all the fine things from London.

The Captain spread out the cargo before the Sultan and his five hundred and fifty-five wives. They were delighted. The Captain of the ship had more African gold to take back to London than ever before.

"Now there is only the cat left," he said to himself. "And for that, I will receive more than its weight in gold!"

While he had been trading with the Sultan, rats and mice had been scurrying about them the whole time, nibbling at sacks, running up curtains and even biting the Sultan's queens. When the Captain went to make his farewells, he went with the cat perched on his shoulder.

In the palace, the mice and rats were squealing and running about as usual. The cat sprang from the Captain's shoulder and in less than five minutes had killed fifty of them and sent the rest to their holes. Then she went and sat at the Sultan's feet, purring, and he ordered a silver dish of thick yellow cream to be set before her.

The Sultan had never seen a cat before, and knew at once that he must have this wonderful creature for his own.

"I shall give you five hundred pieces of gold for the cat," said he, plucking at his turban.

"O Mighty Sultan, may you live forever," replied the Captain. "But if we give up this wonderful cat, the ship will be overrun by rats on our return voyage. They will eat up all the food, and we may starve to death."

"That, indeed, would be a thousand pities," replied the Sultan. "I see that I must give more for the cat to make the risk worth your while. What do you say to a thousand gold pieces and this diamond from my own turban?"

The Captain stared at the diamond, and swallowed. It was as large as a quail's egg and flashing blue fire.

"We will take the risk, O Mighty Sultan," he replied. "The cat is yours."

When the ship came into London docks, all Fitzwarren's men were there to receive the money paid on their Ventures. When it came to Dick's turn, he asked if he could have his cat again, never believing that it had fetched a single gold piece, let alone a fortune. When the Captain told him the tale, Dick could hardly believe him till the Captain showed him the sack of gold and the enormous diamond.

The merchant slapped Dick on the back and called him 'Son Richard'.

"You shall have a share in my next ship," said he. "Lord Mayor of London, eh? Those bells of yours could have spoken truth, it seems!"

Alice had told her father the story of what the bells had said, and he had thought it a good jest. Now, he began to wonder. If this boy could make a fortune out of a single cat, what else might he not do?

Out of his money Dick bought Alice a velvet sash and Cook a silken dress and a silver pin. The rest he ventured in Fitzwarren's next ship, and when the ship returned, Dick was twice as rich. When the ship after that came home, Dick was twice as rich again. By now he was a fine and handsome young man.

"Cook's boy," said Mistress Alice, "you may smile at me now, for I have smiled at you first."

Dick smiled at her. One thing led to another, and soon they were married. The Lord Mayor himself came to the wedding, wearing his red robes and driving in a gilt coach with ten white horses.

"There!" whispered Alice. "See how fine you'll look, Dick, when you're Lord Mayor!"

And ten years later, Dick was Lord Mayor. He went before the King and knelt before him, and the King laid a sword on Dick's shoulder.

"Rise up, Sir Richard!" said he.

So Dick was Sir Richard Whittington, Lord Mayor of London, as the bells had promised him so many years ago as he had leaned on the milestone in the drizzling rain. And sometimes Sir Richard Whittington would still go out of London on a Sunday to that very place, and think about the cat who had made his fortune, and listen again to what the bells were saying:

Turn again Whitting-ton
Thou worthy cit-izen
Lord Mayor of Lon-don!

The Frog Prince

One evening a young princess went into a wood and sat down under a lime tree by a spring of clear water. She had taken with her her favourite plaything, a beautiful golden ball, and kept tossing it idly into the air and catching it again.

Each time she threw it higher and higher, until at last she threw it too high and too far, and missed catching it as it fell. It began to roll away from her, away and away, and before she could run after it, rolled right into the spring itself.

"My ball! O, my ball!" cried the Princess in dismay.

She went and craned right over the edge of the well, but the water was very deep and she knew that she could never reach to the bottom of it. She began to cry, because she had really loved her golden ball, and could not bear to think that she would never play with it again.

"I loved it best of everything in the whole world," she sobbed. "And I'd give anything – everything I've got, to have it back again. All my jewels, all my fine clothes – everything!"

As she finished speaking a frog suddenly put its flat green head out of the water and asked,

"Princess, why do you weep so bitterly?"

"O frog, I have lost my golden ball!" she cried. "It has fallen into the spring and now I shall never see it again!"

"You *may* see it again," replied the frog, "if you let me help you. I heard what you said just now. I do not want your jewels or your fine clothes. But if you will love me, and let me live with you, and eat from your little golden plate and sleep upon your bed, then I will bring you back your ball again."

He sat with his green head cocked and looked at the Princess with his great round eyes, and she looked back at him.

"What nonsense he talks!" thought the Princess. "How could he possibly climb out of the well? And as for coming to live with me at the palace – it's impossible! But he may be able to dive down and fetch my pretty ball, so I'll pretend to promise what he asks."

"Very well, frog," she said out loud. "I will agree to what you ask. And now – dive and fetch me my ball quickly – do!"

So the frog splashed down into the water and disappeared. Next minute he came up again with the ball in his mouth and tossed it to the ground at the Princess's feet.

"O thank you!" cried the Princess, overjoyed. "My ball – my beautiful ball!"

She picked it up and ran gaily off towards the palace, quite forgetting the frog and her own promise.

"Princess, wait!" called the frog after her. "Remember what you promised!"

But the Princess kept on running, and soon was safely home again, her adventure forgotten.

Next day, the Princess was just sitting down to her dinner when there came a strange, soft pattering noise as if slippered feet were coming up the

marble staircase. Sure enough, next moment there came a gentle knocking at the door, and a voice said:

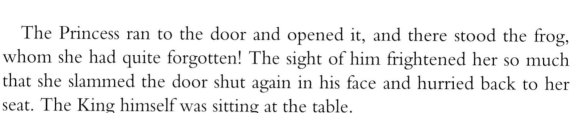

> *"Open the door, my Princess dear,*
> *Open the door to thy true love here!*
> *Remember the words the two of us said*
> *By the fountain cool in the greenwood shade!"*

The Princess ran to the door and opened it, and there stood the frog, whom she had quite forgotten! The sight of him frightened her so much that she slammed the door shut again in his face and hurried back to her seat. The King himself was sitting at the table.

"Who was that at the door?" he asked.

"Only a nasty frog," replied the Princess. "My golden ball fell into the spring yesterday, and he fetched it out for me. But he made me make a silly promise, to let him come here and live with me, and now he's wanting to be let in!"

As she was speaking the frog was knocking at the door again, and saying his sad little song:

> *"Open the door, my Princess dear,*
> *Open the door to thy true love here!*
> *Remember the words the two of us said*
> *By the fountain cool in the greenwood shade!"*

"You must let him in," said the King. "If you made a promise, you must keep it. Open the door."

Much against her will the Princess went and opened the door, and the frog came hopping in and went right over to the table.

"I am hungry," he said to the Princess. "Pray lift me on to a chair, so that I may sit by you."

She did as he asked, though she could hardly bear to touch him, and when she herself had sat down again, he said,

"Push your plate a little closer to me, so that I may eat out of it."

The Princess was forced to obey, though she did not at all like the idea of sharing her plate with a frog.

When he had eaten as much as he could, the frog said, "Now I am tired. Pray carry me upstairs and put me on your own little bed."

The Princess was bound by her promise to do as he asked. She picked up the frog very gingerly, between her fingers, carried him upstairs, and with a shudder dropped him on to her own bed. He crept up on to the pillow, and there he slept all night long. But when morning came, he jumped up and hopped down the stairs and out of the palace.

"Thank heaven!" cried the Princess. "Now he has gone, and I shall see no more of him."

But she was mistaken. That night as she sat at table there came again that same soft slippery footstep on the stair, and that same gentle knocking at the door. Once again the Princess was forced to feed the frog from her own golden plate, and take him up to her own bed to sleep.

On the third night, when again the frog visited her, the Princess began to regret her promise bitterly.

But on the third morning when she woke, it was to find the frog gone already from her pillow. And there, standing at the foot of the bed, was the most handsome prince she had ever seen, gazing at her with eyes that were loving and gentle and strangely like those of the little frog.

"Dear Princess!" cried the Prince. "You have broken the spell at last!"

He told her how he had been enchanted by a wicked fairy. She had

41

changed him into a frog, and told him that he would never again take human shape unless he could find a Princess who would take him from the spring and bring him home with her, to feed from her own plate and sleep upon her bed.

"And now you have done this," cried the Prince, "and I love you dearly, and want you to come with me to my own kingdom and marry me, and be my queen."

And so it happened. Next day the Princess drove off with her Prince in a fine golden coach drawn by six white horses, bound for his own kingdom, where they married and lived happily ever after.

Puss in Boots

Once upon a time there was a poor Miller who had three sons. When he died he had nothing to leave them but his mill, his ass and his cat. So he left the mill to his eldest son, the ass to his second son, and his youngest son had to be contented with the cat.

"Whatever shall I do?" cried he. "It's all very well for my brothers, but once I've killed my cat and sold his skin to make gloves, I'll have nothing at all in the world!"

Master Puss heard all this.

"Sell my skin to make gloves?" he mewed. "You can do better than this with me, dear Master. In fact, if you do everything that I tell you, there's a fortune to be made!"

The young man was very surprised and pleased to find that he had such a clever cat, and readily agreed to do as he was bid.

"First," said Puss, "find me a pair of stout leather boots, and a sack."

The Miller's son found both and brought them to him, and Puss drew on the great boots with a loud purring and swaggered up and down to show them off. He then slung the sack over his shoulder and went into the nearby countryside.

He stopped at last in a field that was full of rabbit warrens, and laid down the sack by the largest burrow. Then Puss himself lay down by the sack with his head hanging limply to one side as if he had broken his neck.

After a time, up came a fine fat rabbit, saw the 'dead' cat, and went sniffing into the sack to find the bran and lettuce leaves that Puss had placed there. Up jumped Puss, pulled the strings of the sack tight, and the rabbit was caught.

That evening Puss came to the door of the palace carrying a brace of plump rabbits, and demanded to see the King. The Chamberlain was charmed by the sight of this impudent Puss in his fine boots, and led the way to the throne room.

Puss made a sweeping bow and laid the rabbits at the King's feet, saying,

"Your Majesty, here is a gift from my master, My Lord the Marquis of Carabas!"

The King was delighted both with the gift and with Puss himself, and gave orders that the cat was to be allowed to call whenever he pleased.

Puss purred. This suited him very well. Each day he went poaching in the king's woods and each evening he went to the palace with his catch and offered it to the King as 'a gift from My Lord the Marquis of Carabas'. Besides this, the Miller's son had as many rabbits and pheasants as he wanted, as well as the presents that Puss brought back from the King himself.

One day Puss came back from the palace in great excitement.

"O Master, Master!" he mewed. "The time has come for your fortune to be made! Just do as I tell you, and all will be well. All you have to do is to go down and bathe in the river. At noon, the King will ride by with his only child, the Princess. You must be in the water when they arrive. Don't be alarmed whatever should happen, and leave it all to me!"

By now the Miller's son was ready to do anything his cat asked, and so next day he went down to the river as he had been told. There he stripped off his worn and ragged clothes and plunged into the water. As soon as he had done so, Puss ran up, took the heap of clothes, and hid them in a ditch. Then he waited till he heard the wheels of the king's carriage and ran out on to the road crying, "Help! Help! My Master, the Marquis of Carabas is drowning!"

When the King saw it was his favourite, the Puss in Boots who brought him so many presents, he ordered his servants to hurry to the river.

"Alas, alas!" cried the cunning Puss as he led the way. "Wicked robbers set upon my Master and robbed him of his fine clothes and jewels and everything he had. Then they threw him into the river to drown, and I myself cannot swim. Save him, quickly, before he drowns! O my dear Master!"

The servants ran and pulled the Miller's son out of the water and one of them went running back to the palace to fetch a suit of the King's own clothes. Puss led him to the King and introduced him as 'My most noble Master, My Lord the Marquis of Carabas.' The King was so charmed by his noble appearance that he invited him into the carriage to join himself and the Princess on their ride. Puss purred.

But there was still work to be done. Puss ran on ahead, tail up in the air, till he came to a field of corn where men were haymaking.

"Good people!" cried Puss, his whiskers curling, "Soon the King is coming this way. He is sure to stop and ask who this fine field belongs to. And if you do not say that it belongs to My Lord the Marquis of Carabas, I will have you all chopped up as small as mincemeat!"

Off he bounded, and when the king stopped to admire the hay and ask to whom it belonged, all the men in the field replied,

"It belongs to My Lord the Marquis of Carabas!"

"What fine hay you have, Marquis," said the King, and the Miller's son bowed politely.

By this time, Puss himself had reached a great cornfield where men were cutting the ripe corn with sickles and binding it into sheaves. Puss called out to them, and they were so amazed to see a Puss in boots that they too obeyed his orders, and when the King stopped to ask to whom the corn belonged, meekly replied,

"It belongs to My Lord the Marquis of Carabas!"

Meanwhile, Puss had come to the castle where lived the wicked Ogre who was the real owner of all the land about. He was so cruel that anyone who disobeyed him was straightway killed and served up for the Ogre's dinner. No one could fight him, because he had the power of turning himself into any animal he chose – and no one could fight single-handed against a savage tiger or raging wolf.

Puss came striding up to the castle gates, bared his teeth at the guards and went straight into the hall where the Ogre sat.

"What's this?" growled the Ogre, chewing at a bone. "Who are you, and how dare you enter my castle?"

"O Your Eminence, O Your Excellency, O Your *Most* Excellency," mewed Puss, bowing so low that his ears brushed the ground, "I am a traveller, out to see the wonders of the world. And of all the wonders of the world, I have heard that you are the wonderfullest. Ever since I was a kitten I have heard tales of you that I could scarcely believe. They say you can change yourself into any animal you choose. Is it true? I can hardly believe it!"

"Believe it!" cried the Ogre, crunching his bone, "Believe it! I'll show you!"

Next minute, there stood a great yellow lion lashing its tail and roaring, and Puss himself was up in the rafters, arching his back and spitting.

The Ogre changed back into his own shape again, bellowing with laughter, and Puss came carefully down from the roof.

"O sir, O noble and mighty Sir," cried Puss, "Forgive me for not believing! Now I have seen it with my own eyes, I see how truly wonderful you are. But there is one *tiny* thing that worries me."

"What?" roared the Ogre, tearing the leg from a roast ox. "What, miserable little cat?"

"Please, sir, noble, sir," said Puss. "You are so noble and fine that to be able to change yourself into a lion, the king of the beasts himself, is almost to be expected. But how could so great and powerful a person as yourself change himself into some very small and humble creature, such as a mouse, for instance? That, I'm sure is quite impossible!"

"Impossible?" yelled the Ogre, snapping the ox bone in half. "Wretched little creature, I'll show you!"

A moment later the Ogre was gone and a small brown mouse scampered over the floor. Puss poised, ears back, tail a-twitch, pounced – and gobbled the mouse in a trice. And that was the end of the Ogre. Puss purred.

All the Ogre's servants came running into the hall, laughing and crying for joy. Puss jumped up on to a table and held up a paw for silence.

"I have killed your cruel master," he said, "and now a new master is coming who will treat you wisely and well. But if you do not do as I tell you, I will have you all chopped as small as mincemeat!"

This the people could readily believe.

"All you have to do," said Puss, "is to tell the King when he enquires, that this castle and all its lands belong to My Lord the Marquis of Carabas!"

And so, when evening came and the King's coach came rolling out of the sunset and over the drawbridge, hundreds of servants in rich liveries stood in lines on either side. Puss came forward and opened the carriage door with a sweeping bow.

"Welcome, Your Majesty!" he mewed. "Welcome to the castle of My Lord the Marquis of Carabas!"

"This too?" cried the King, astonished, looking about him at the magnificent castle and throngs of servants. "Truly, sir, you are worthy to be a member of the royal family!"

Puss hid a smile behind his paw and led the way indoors where a splendid banquet was prepared. At the end of it the King, who had noticed that the Princess and the young man were holding hands under the table, wiped his mouth on a napkin, hiccoughed happily, and said,

"Marquis, I know of no one whom I would rather have for a son-in-law than yourself. I can see that my daughter likes you, and if she is willing, let the wedding take place immediately."

The Miller's youngest son held his breath. Was he really to become a Prince – perhaps a King?

Then "I will marry him gladly," replied the king's daughter.

Puss purred.

Rapunzel

A man and his wife both longed to have a child. As years went by and still there was no sign of one, they began to despair. But one day the wife was down by the stream washing clothes when a frog put his head out of the water and told her that soon her wish was to be granted.

The wife was overjoyed, and hurried home to tell her husband, who immediately set about making a wooden cradle ready for the baby.

Now next to the cottage where these two lived was a great, overgrown garden, belonging to a strange old woman whom they had hardly ever seen. People said she was a witch, and were afraid of her.

One day the wife was peering over the wall into this garden when she saw a clump of green rampion growing there. Immediately she began to long for a taste of it, though she had never been very fond of it before.

"Dear husband, I must eat some rampion or die!" she told him when he came home from working in the forest. "Climb over the wall and fetch me some, I beg you."

The husband did not like the idea at all.

"It doesn't belong to us," he told her. "And as for that old woman who owns the garden, for all we know she may be a witch, and if she catches me out – what then?"

"What nonsense!" cried the wife. "Witch indeed! I must have some rampion, I tell you, or I shall die!"

And so the man, although he knew full well that the old woman *was* a witch, waited until twilight and then climbed softly over the wall and began to pull up the rampion as quickly as he could. But when he straightened up to climb back over the wall, he found himself face to face with the old witch herself, eyes a-glitter in the gloom.

"How *dare* you climb into my garden and tear up my plants!" she cried in a terrible voice. "I have caught you red-handed, and now it will be the worse for you!"

The poor man, shaking and trembling, explained how greatly his wife had longed for the rampion, and begged the witch to forgive him.

"Never!" she cried. "But I will make a bargain with you. Your wife is about to have a child. I will let you go free and take with you as much rampion as you like, on condition that when the child is born *I* shall have it, to bring up as my own."

The man agreed, for he was so terrified that he hardly knew what he was saying, and scrambled safely back over the wall with the stolen rampion and a heavy heart.

Soon afterwards, a daughter was born, and when she was only a few days old the witch came and carried the child off with her. She gave her the name Rapunzel (which is another name for rampion).

When Rapunzel was twelve years old the witch locked her in a tall stone tower that stood in the thickest and darkest part of a great wood. It had neither staircase nor doors, only a little window in Rapunzel's own room right at the very top.

Whenever the witch wanted to enter, she would stand below and call up,

"Rapunzel, Rapunzel, let down your hair!"

Rapunzel had long yellow hair, which she wore in plaits wound about her head. When she heard the witch, she would twist them round a hook by the window and let them down. They fell like thick golden ropes, and the witch would climb up by them.

When Rapunzel had been in the tower for several years it happened one day that the king's son rode by. He heard a beautiful voice singing nearby, and pushing his way through the dim green thicket came for the first time upon the lonely sunless tower. Rapunzel's voice drifted down from the little window, and she sang so sweetly of her loneliness that the Prince longed to join her. He searched about the tower to find a door, but in vain, and in the end he was forced to ride away.

After that, he would often ride in the wood and make his way to the tower in its secret thicket. And one day, while he was hidden there among the laurel leaves, the old witch herself appeared, and he heard her call out,

"Rapunzel, Rapunzel, let down your hair!"

The Prince saw Rapunzel's face at the high window, he saw her lift her hands to unpin her braids, and a minute later the golden ropes of hair came tumbling to the ground. The witch climbed up while the Prince watched.

"If that is the ladder that will take me up to that fair lady, then I shall try my own luck," he thought.

Next day he went at evening into the forest and came to the tower in the half darkness. He called from the shadow of the thicket in a voice as hoarse as the witch's own,

"Rapunzel, Rapunzel, let down your hair!"

Then at last he was grasping the smooth warm ropes of hair and climbing upwards and into the little stone room.

Rapunzel was terrified when first she saw him, for she had never so much as set eyes on a man before. But the Prince spoke gently to her, telling how he had come each day to hear her sing, and how his heart had been won by her song. When he told her that he wished to take her away and marry her, he looked so kind and handsome that she could not help thinking, "He is better by far than old Mother Gothel, and surely he will love me better."

So she put her hand in his, and said "Yes".

"But I cannot escape without a ladder," she said. "So each time you come, you must bring with you a skein of silk. I will weave it into a ladder, and when it is long enough, then I shall climb down by it, and you can take me away on your horse."

"I will come every day," the Prince promised.

"But you must come in the evening," Rapunzel told him. "Old Mother Gothel comes in the daytime, and so she will never discover you."

And so the Prince began to visit Rapunzel every evening, and they would sit together in the twilight while Rapunzel sang and wove her silken ladder. And all would have been well for them if one day Rapunzel had not said to the witch, quite without thinking,

"How is it, Mother Gothel, that you are twice as heavy to draw up as the young Prince who comes at evening?"

No sooner were the words out than Rapunzel saw her mistake, and clapped her hand to her mouth with a little cry. But it was too late.

"What is that you say?" cried the witch in a fury. "Wicked girl, – have you deceived me?"

And she seized Rapunzel's beautiful hair in one hand and with the other snatched up a pair of shears and cut off the long plaits in two fierce snips. They fell to the floor in shining coils.

Rapunzel's tears and pleas were all in vain. The merciless witch spirited her from the stone tower to a far-off wilderness, where she left her to wander all alone and fend for herself.

Then, at evening, the old witch fastened the plaits of hair to the hook by the window, and waited. Sure enough, as the light faded, the Prince came riding into the thicket and she heard him call,

"Rapunzel, Rapunzel, let down your hair!"

With an evil smile she let the long ropes fall.

The Prince climbed eagerly upward and in his joy he did not notice that the golden ropes were cold as ice between his hands. He swung over the stone sill into the little room and was face to face with the towering witch.

"So you've come to visit your lady love!" she shrieked. "But the pretty bird has flown, my dear, the cat has got her, and she'll sing no more, I promise you! And as for you, the cat shall scratch out *your* eyes, too! Rapunzel is gone forever, and you shall never set eyes on her again!"

At this the Prince was so beside himself with grief and despair that he threw himself down from the window. He fell into the dark thicket, and though he was not killed, the sharp thorns scratched out his eyes and he was left in darkness.

Alone and blind he wandered the woods, living on roots and berries and lamenting the loss of his bride. Years and years went by, until at last he came to that very wilderness where Rapunzel had been cast by the witch and where she was still living.

As he went in darkness he heard a sweet voice singing and knew instantly that he had found Rapunzel, and called her name out loud.

She came running to him and fell into his arms, weeping. Two of her warm tears fell upon his eyes and in that moment he could see as well as ever before, and the very first thing he saw with his new eyes was Rapunzel's face.

Then he took her away to his own kingdom where they were welcomed with great rejoicing and married at last, to live long and happily together.

The Sleeping Beauty

There once lived a King and Queen who were married for many years without having any children. Then at last a daughter was born to them, and so delighted were they that they gave a feast for the baby's christening. Invitations were sent to all the lords and ladies in the land and to far off kings and queens.

Thirteen fairies lived in this kingdom, but the King had only twelve golden plates to set before them, and so he had to leave one of the fairies out.

On the day of the christening the King and his guests feasted merrily, and in the evening before they left, all the fairies presented the Princess with a magic gift. One gave her the gift of wisdom, another the gift of beauty, a third wished her all the riches she desired. And so it went on until the eleventh fairy had spoken, when suddenly the glittering crowd of guests parted and between them went the thirteenth fairy, all in black.

She looked neither left nor right and greeted no one. She stopped by the side of the baby's cradle and lifted her arms like great black wings and cried in a terrible voice, "When the Princess is fifteen years old, she shall prick herself with a spindle and fall down dead!"

Her arms fell and in a great silence she turned and went out of the hall.

Now the twelfth fairy still had not made her gift. It was beyond her power to undo the wicked spell entirely, but she was able to soften it, by saying, "When the Princess pricks herself with a spindle, she shall not die, but fall into a deep sleep lasting for a hundred years."

Even this seemed tragedy enough to the King and Queen, and they gave orders that all the spindles in the land should be burned. As the Princess grew up, growing wiser and lovelier and kinder each day, the fairy's curse began to seem very faint and far away, so that they hardly thought of it at all.

On the Princess's fifteenth birthday a party was held at the Palace. The Princess begged for a game of hide-and-seek. The guests scattered and the Princess herself began to run up and down the stone corridors, looking for a hiding place. At last she came to a crumbling tower that she had never noticed before.

"They will never find me here!" she thought.

She climbed the narrow, winding stairs and came to a studded door with a great rusty key in the lock. The Princess turned it and went inside.

There in the cold stone room sat an old woman with a spindle, spinning flax. The Princess stared. All the spindles in the kingdom had disappeared long ago, because of the fairy's curse, and so she had never set eyes on one before.

"Good day, Granny," said the Princess. She had quite forgotten the game of hide-and-seek. "What are you doing?"

"I am spinning," replied the old woman, nodding her head.

"And what is this that whirls round so merrily?" asked the Princess. With these words she took the spindle and tried to spin too.

But she had scarcely touched it before the curse was fulfilled and she pricked her finger with the spindle. She fell back on to the bed nearby, and the old woman, her work done, went away down the stone stairs with her evil laughter echoing about her.

At the very moment when the Princess fell to the bed her guests, too, closed their eyes and slept just where they happened to be – some in cupboards, some behind pillars and others under the great four poster beds. Even the King and Queen fell asleep in the great hall. Their courtiers yawned and rubbed their eyes and soon were sprawling on the strewn rushes. The horses lay sleeping in the stables, the dogs in the yard, the doves on the roof, the flies on the wall. Even the fire on the hearth stopped its flickering and the meat on the spit stopped crackling. The cook, who was about to box the scullion's ears, began to snore with her arm still raised for the blow. Outside, the wind dropped. Not a bough stirred, not a twig, not a leaf. All slept.

Round the castle a hedge of briers began to grow up, minute by minute. It grew higher and higher, surrounding the whole castle with live green walls of thorn and bramble. Soon nothing could be seen from the outside world, not even a turret, not even a flag on the roof. Within, the clocks ticked to a standstill, the dust settled, there was nothing but sleep and silence.

A legend grew up as years went by about the sleeping Brier Rose, as the Princess was called. Princes came from far off lands to try to force their way through the high thickets. But the greedy thorns clutched them like hands so that they could never escape and were left there to die.

Then, one day, when the hundred years were nearly up, a bold and handsome prince rode by. He met an old man working in the woods, who told him the legend of the beautiful sleeping Princess. He begged the Prince not to try to enter, and warned him of the terrible fate that had befallen the rest.

"I am not afraid," replied the Prince. "I am determined to go and see Brier Rose with my own eyes."

He rode to the thicket, never knowing that this very day the one hundred years were ended, and the Princess would wake from her spellbound sleep. As the Prince drew near, he saw to his astonishment that the hedge was covered with large and beautiful flowers. They seemed to be unfurling their petals even as he watched. As he rode up the briers curled back and made way for him so that he could pass unharmed, and then closed up again into a hedge behind him.

In the courtyard he found brindled dogs lying asleep, nose on paws. He saw doves on the roof, heads under wings. He pushed the door and entered the silent palace and saw there the King and Queen themselves, lying by the throne. The Prince had to step over the sleeping forms of guards and courtiers and passed next through the kitchen where the cook had stood for a hundred years with her arm raised ready to box the scullion's ears. Nearby sat a maid who had been fixed in time while she plucked the black feathers from a fowl on her knee.

The Prince went tiptoe through all the palace, and so great was the hush that he could hear his own breathing. Then at last he came to the ancient tower and climbing the winding stair came to the chamber where Brier Rose lay sleeping.

The Princess looked so beautiful lying there that the Prince knelt by the bedside and kissed her gently on the lips. And to his wonder, Brier Rose opened her eyes and gazed up at him. Then she sat up and yawned.

And then she stretched and asked the time of day for all the world as if she had woken from a nap.

The Prince and Brier Rose went down together and found the whole palace astir. The hounds sprang up and wagged their tails, the doves on the roof stretched their wings and fluttered off to the fields. The flies buzzed, the fire leapt, the meat began to roast. And the scullion received at last the box on the ears that had threatened him for a hundred years, and let out a yell that woke the maid who was plucking the fowl.

Everything went on as if nothing had ever happened, as if a century were no more than the twinkling of an eye. And soon the dust of a hundred years was flying in clouds through open doors and windows as the palace was prepared for the wedding of Brier Rose and her gallant prince.

Snow White
and the Seven Dwarfs

A Queen sat sewing by the window one day when the snow was falling. She lifted her head to see a raven walking on the white lawns, and as she did so, pricked her finger. A drop of blood fell, and in that moment the Queen made a wish.

"I wish that I might have a little daughter, and that her skin might be as white as snow, her lips red as blood and her hair black as a raven's wing."

She spoke the wish out loud and when she had finished the raven spread his black wings and flew off into the swirling snow.

Not long afterwards a daughter was born to the King and Queen, and the Queen, remembering her wish, called the child Snow White. And as she grew older her skin was white as snow, her lips were red as blood and her hair shone like a raven's wing.

After a few years the Queen died and the King married again. His new wife was beautiful and proud. She would gaze and gaze at herself in the magic glass that hung in her room, and say to it,

> *"Mirror, Mirror on the wall,*
> *Who is the fairest of us all?"*

Then the glass would answer,

> *"Pale as the moon, bright as a star,*
> *Thou art the fairest, Queen by far!"*

And the Queen would smile at her reflection in the cold glass and stretch her neck like a swan and preen.

But Snow White grew more and more beautiful each day, and when she was seven years old she was even fairer than the Queen herself.

The magic mirror could not tell a lie, and so when next the Queen asked it,

> *"Mirror, Mirror on the wall,*
> *Who is the fairest of us all?"*

the reply came,

> *"Fair as the day, O Queen, you are,*
> *But Snow White is lovelier by far!"*

At this the Queen turned white with rage. She sent for a huntsman and told him to take Snow White deep into the forest and there to kill her. But when the huntsman drew his knife to plunge it into her heart, and Snow White began to cry and beg for her life, he remembered his own children at home, and slowly let the knife fall.

"Run as far off as you can," he told her. "If ever you return, we shall both lose our lives."

Then he turned and left her, and on his way back to the palace he killed a fawn and cut out its heart to take back to the Queen, pretending it was Snow White's.

Now Snow White was alone in the dim green forest and as she ran the brambles clutched at her dress like live hands and the sharp stones cut into her feet. Then, in the dusk, she came upon a little house, the first she had seen all day, and because she was so tired, went inside to rest.

Inside, everything was very small and yet neat and clean as could be. There was a small table set out with a white cloth and seven little plates and seven little loaves and seven little glasses with wine in them. By the wall were seven little beds, neatly made.

Snow White was so hungry that she went right round the table taking a little nibble from each plate and a sip of wine from each glass.

Then, because she was so tired after her day in the forest, she went to the row of beds and tried first one and then another till she found the most comfortable. She lay down and went straight to sleep.

Soon afterwards, the owners of the house came home. They were seven dwarfs, who worked all day deep in the mountainside with pick and shovel, digging for gold and precious stones. Once inside, they lit the lamps and saw at once that things were not as they had left them.

"Who has been sitting in my chair?" said the first.

"Who has been using my fork?" said the second.

"Who has been nibbling my bread?" said the third.

"Who has been picking at my vegetables?" said the fourth.

"Who has been drinking out of my glass?" said the fifth.

"Who has been cutting with my knife?" said the sixth.

"And who has been eating off my plate?" said the seventh.

Then one of them went over to his bed and saw a dent in the covers and he cried, "Someone has been sitting on my bed!"

Then all the rest ran up to their beds crying, "And mine! And mine!" until the seventh dwarf went to *his* bed and found Snow White herself, fast asleep.

"Sssssh!" he hissed loudly to the others. "Sssh! Come and look!"

All seven dwarfs crowded round the bed whispering and nudging one another and all fixing their eyes on Snow White's beautiful face.

"What a lovely child!" they whispered. "We mustn't wake her!"

So all through the night the seven dwarfs took turns to watch by Snow White's bedside, an hour each until morning came. When she awoke and saw the seven dwarfs, Snow White was frightened and covered her eyes. But they spoke gently to her and asked her name and how she had come there alone through the thick forest. Snow White told them her story, and when she had finished the first dwarf asked, "Can you cook and sew and spin? Can you dust and sweep and kindle fires? Can you knit and bake and can you trim a lamp?"

Snow White could do all these things, because her stepmother had kept her hard at work at home. And so the dwarfs said that she could stay with them and look after the house while they went off each day to dig for gold and silver in the mountains.

Each day, before they set off in the grey dawn the dwarfs would warn Snow White.

"Take care to let no one in. One day the Queen will find out where you are and try to harm you."

All this time the Queen had thought Snow White was dead, and was so sure that she was now the most beautiful in the land that she had not troubled to use her magic glass. But one day, when she had nothing else to do, she went and sat before it, smiled at her reflection and asked,

"Mirror, Mirror on the wall,
Who is the fairest of us all?"

And the glass answered,

"Queen, thou art the fairest here, I hold,
But in the forest and over fell
Snow White with the seven dwarfs doth dwell
And she is fairer, a thousandfold!"

At this the Queen was mad with hate and envy, and lifted her arm to

shatter the mirror into a thousand pieces. But her arm fell, and she thought, "No. It is not the mirror I must destroy, but Snow White!"

Next day she stained her face brown and dressed in rags like a pedlar woman and set off into the forest to the cottage of the seven dwarfs. There she stood beneath the window with her big hat shading her face and called out, "Wares to sell! Wares to sell!"

Snow White put her head out of the window.

"Good day," she said. "What have you to sell?"

"Pretty trinkets," replied the wicked Queen. "And coloured laces for your waist!"

She held up one of plaited scarlet silk, dangling it under Snow White's eyes so that she thought, "Surely I may let this pedlar in? She seems kind and honest, and has such pretty things!"

She opened the door and the Queen went in.

"Gracious, child!" she cried. "How badly your dress is laced! Here let *me* do it, with this pretty scarlet lace, and you shall have it for a penny!"

Snow White stood quite still while the pedlar threaded the new red lace with nimble fingers. But the wicked Queen pulled the laces tighter and tighter and tighter till at last all the breath was squeezed out of Snow White's body and she fell to the floor as if she were dead.

"That's the end of *you* and your beauty!" cried the spiteful Queen, and hastened back towards the palace.

When the dwarfs came back and found Snow White lying lifeless on the floor they guessed at once what had happened. One of them seized a knife and cut the scarlet lace and at once Snow White drew in a great sigh and began to breathe again. The dwarfs gave a shout of joy, and next day when they set off in the mists for the mountains they begged her to take care, and be on the watch for the wicked Queen.

That very morning the Queen herself rose early and went to the magic mirror.

"Mirror, Mirror on the wall,
Who is the fairest of us all?"

When the mirror gave the same answer as before the Queen could not speak for anger. In terrible silence she dressed in a disguise, a different one, and took up a tray of pretty combs and painted one of them with deadly poison. She set off to the dwarfs' house and there she knocked on the door and cried, "Fine wares to sell! Fine wares to sell!"

Again Snow White looked through the window, and said, "I cannot open the door – I dare not. I have promised to let no one in!"

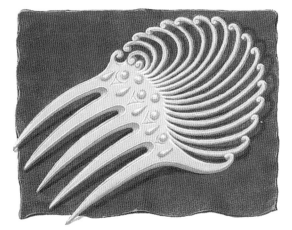

"There is no need to open the door," replied the Queen. "Just look at my beautiful combs."

She picked out a carved comb of finest ivory. Snow White put it into her hair and no sooner had she done so than she fell to the floor in a deadly swoon.

"There you may lie!" cried the wicked Queen, and went her way.

Luckily, that day the dwarfs came home from the mountains early and found Snow White before she was quite dead. They gently took the poisoned comb from her hair and after a time she opened her eyes and sat up. When she told them what had happened they warned her yet again to beware, and again Snow White promised that she would.

That very night the Queen went to her magic mirror again. When she received the same reply as before and knew that Snow White must still be living she shivered and shook from head to foot with rage. She pointed her long white finger into the mirror and it pointed back at her.

"Snow White shall die!" she cried. "Even if it costs *my* life!"

All night long she secretly worked at a poisoned apple. One side of it was rosy and shining, the other clear and green. Whoever took a bite from the red side was sure to die.

At dawn the Queen went gliding out to the woods dressed as a peasant's wife. When she came to the dwarfs' house she knocked and Snow White put her head out of the window.

"I cannot open the door," she said. "The dwarfs have made me promise not to."

"Very well," said the old woman. "It doesn't matter to me whether you do or not. But perhaps you'd like this apple as a present before I go?"

Snow White shook her head.

"What is the matter?" asked the peasant woman. "Do you think that it is poisoned? Silly girl – see, watch me!"

She turned the green side of the apple to her lips and bit into it.

"There!" said she. "If it were poisoned, do you think *I* should have eaten it? Here, take the rest and eat it!"

Snow White longed for the shining red apple with its juicy flesh. She took it from the old woman, bit into the rosy skin and fell to the ground.

"This time nothing shall save her!" cried the Queen, and hastened back to the castle. There she went and stood before the magic mirror and at last it gave her the answer she wanted,

"Thou art the fairest, Queen, by far!"

When the dwarfs came home, they found Snow White lying there and did everything they could think of to bring her back to life. It was in vain. Snow White's eyelids never flickered, not the faintest breath floated from her lips. For seven days and seven nights they watched by her side, but there was not the least stir of life. For all that, Snow White was still so beautiful that they could hardly bring themselves to believe that she was really dead.

"We can't bury her in the cold ground!" they cried. And they made a coffin of glass and placed her in it and wrote her name on it in gold letters. They carried the coffin to the hillside and one of the dwarfs always sat by it and watched, day and night.

Snow White lay many years on the bare mountain side and still she seemed only to sleep. Her lips were red as blood, her skin was white as snow and her hair black as a raven's wing just as they had been in life.

It happened one day that a prince came riding by and saw Snow White within her glass walls. He read the gold lettering and learned her name, and that she was the daughter of a king.

"Give her to me!" he begged the dwarfs. But they all shook their heads and refused to let her go.

"I will give you gold and treasure," pleaded the Prince.

Again they refused.

"We will not give her up for all the treasure in the world!"

"Then I shall stay here on the mountain all my days looking on Snow White," said the Prince. "I cannot live without her."

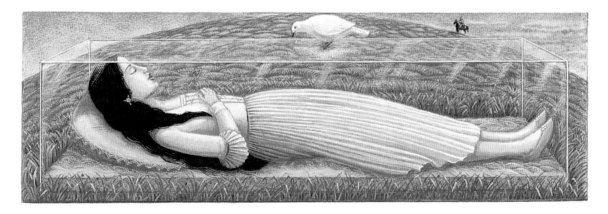

At this, the dwarfs pitied him and could not deny him what he asked. They themselves helped to lift the coffin, and as they did so, the piece of poisoned apple fell from Snow White's lips. She opened her eyes, lifted her head, and cried in astonishment, "What's happening?"

The Prince, overjoyed, lifted her from the coffin and told her the story of how she had been poisoned by the wicked Queen and had lain like one dead for more than seven years.

"But now you have come to life again," he said. "And I love you better than all the world. Come with me to my father's kingdom and marry me!"

And so Snow White said farewell to the seven dwarfs and went with the Prince to his father's castle where a great feast was prepared for their wedding. Among the guests invited was Snow White's wicked stepmother. She dressed herself in her finest clothes and when she was ready, stood before the magic glass and smiled proudly.

> *"Mirror, Mirror on the wall,*
> *Who is the fairest of us all?"*

And the glass replied,
> *"Fair as the day, O Queen, you are,*
> *But the new bride is lovelier, by far!"*

At this the Queen's fury was so great that she lifted her jewelled hand and struck the glass and it broke into a thousand pieces. Then she went out and rode to the wedding, so that she could see with her own eyes this bride who was even more beautiful than herself.

And when she went into the hall and saw that the bride was none other than Snow White, she flew into such a passion of hate and envy that her heart burst and she fell down dead.

But Snow White and the Prince were married that day and lived and reigned happily ever after.

Snow-white and Rose-red

There was once a poor widow who lived in a lonely cottage. In the garden were two rose trees, and one of them bore white and the other red flowers. She had two daughters and one was called Snow-white and the other Rose-red.

The children were so fond of each other that they went everywhere together. When Snow-white said, "We will not leave each other," Rose-red would answer, "Never so long as we live," and their mother would add, "What one has she must share with the other."

And that was how it was. In summer they ran about the forest alone and no harm ever came to them. On winter evenings when the snow fell the mother would read aloud and the two girls listened as they sat and spun. By them lay a white lamb and above them perched a white dove.

One evening there came a knock at the door. The mother said, "Quick, Rose-red, open the door. It must be a traveller seeking shelter."

But when Rose-red opened the door she saw not a man but a great black bear.

Rose-red screamed, the lamb bleated, the dove fluttered and Snow-white hid under the bed, but the bear said, "Do not be afraid, I will do you no harm. I am half frozen and only want to warm myself a little."

"Poor bear," said the mother. "Lie down by the fire, but take care you do not burn your coat."

So out the girls came and fetched a broom and knocked the snow out of the bear's thick coat, and he stretched himself by the fire and growled contentedly. The lamb and dove came near him and were not afraid.

Soon the children began to play games with their clumsy guest. They climbed all over him and rolled him about and beat him with a stick till he cried,

"Snowy-white, Rosey-red,
Will you beat your lover dead?"

The bear stayed all night by the fire and then at dawn he shambled over the snow into the forest. After that, he came every evening at the same time and the door was never locked until he came. When it was spring and everywhere was green the bear said one morning, "Now I must go away into the forest, to guard my treasures from the wicked dwarfs. In winter when the ground is frozen they are forced to stay down below. But when the sun has warmed the earth up they come to pry and steal!"

The girls were sorry to see him go and often wandered in the forest hoping that they might meet him. Then one day they did find someone, but it was not the bear. It was a dwarf with withered face and red eyes and snow white beard a yard long. The end of the beard was trapped in the crevice of a fallen tree and he was jumping up and down trying to free it. When he saw the children he called, "Why do you stand there? Do something! Help me!"

The girls tried very hard, and all the while he scolded them and called them names. In the end Snow-white took out her scissors and cut off the end of the beard.

The minute he was free the dwarf snatched up a bag of gold that lay nearby and instead of thanking them said, "Stupid goose! Cutting off my fine beard! Bad luck to you!" Off he went, still grumbling.

Soon after that Snow-white and Rose-red were by the stream when they saw something like a large grasshopper jumping by the water. They ran to it and found it was the dwarf. A big fish had bit and the dwarf's beard was caught in the line. The fish was twice as big as the dwarf and would soon have pulled him into the water. Out came the scissors and again – snip! Off came part of the beard.

The dwarf said not a word of thanks for his rescue.

"Dolt! Toadstool! Now you have spoilt my beard!"

He snatched up a sack of pearls that lay among the rushes and made off.

A third time Rose-red and Snow-white met that dwarf. This time he had been caught up in the claws of an eagle, and was screaming in terror. The girls ran and took tight hold of him and pulled and at last the eagle let him go.

"Clumsy things!" yelled the dwarf. "You have dragged at my brown coat and torn it!"

He grabbed a sack of precious stones and scuttled off behind a stone.

The two girls went on, but in the evening they passed the same place again. There was the dwarf, who had emptied out his bag of precious stones to count and gloat over them. They glittered and shone in the evening sun. The dwarf saw the girls and his ashen face glowed red with rage.

"Why do you stand gaping there?" he cried.

Just then there came a loud growling and out of the forest lumbered a great black bear. The dwarf sprang back in fright and begged the bear to spare him.

"Take these two wicked girls instead! They're plump and tender morsels! Eat them!"

The bear gave the wicked creature a single blow with his paw. The dwarf did not move again. The girls were terrified and were going to run off when the bear said, "Snow-white and Rose-red, do not be afraid!"

As he spoke, the bearskin fell off, and there stood a handsome man, clothed all in gold.

"I am a king's son," he said. "I was bewitched by that wicked dwarf who has stolen all my treasures. I had to run about the forest as a bear until I was freed by his death. Now he has his well-deserved punishment."

Snow-white was married to him and Rose-red to his brother, and they divided between them the treasure the dwarf had heaped in his dark cave. The old mother lived happily with her children for many years. She took the two rose trees with her, and they stood before her window and every year bore beautiful roses, white and red.

The Twelve Dancing Princesses

Long ago there was a king who had twelve beautiful daughters. They slept in two great beds in one room, and each night the door of this room was shut and locked. But every morning when the Princesses were woken, their shoes were found to be quite worn out. It was as if the Princesses had been out walking – or dancing? – all night long, and yet how could this possibly be? Nobody could think of an answer to the mystery, and as for the Princesses themselves, they simply smiled and said not a single word.

Then the King proclaimed throughout the land that if anyone could discover the secret, then he could choose whichever of the Princesses he liked best to become his wife, and he should become King himself when the old King died. But if anyone should try for three days and three nights and still did not succeed, then he should be put to death.

Before long a handsome Prince arrived at the court to try his luck. He was given a room next to the Princesses' own, and when he went to bed, he left the door open, so that nothing could take place without his knowing it. He lay down on his bed, determined to stay awake all night and watch. But despite himself he soon fell asleep, and when he woke it was to find that it was already morning and the Princesses' shoes, as usual, were quite worn out, their soles tattered and full of holes. The same thing happened again on the second night and on the third, and so the King, true to his word, ordered the young man's head to be cut off.

Several more suitors came to try their luck, but exactly the same thing happened to them, too, and they all lost their heads.

Now it happened that an old soldier, who had been wounded in battle and could fight no longer, was passing through the country where this king reigned. And as he was travelling through a wood he met an old woman who asked him where he was going.

"That I hardly know," replied the soldier. "But what I should like best in the world would be to find out where it is that the Princesses dance at night. Because then I should become king one day, and that I *would* like!"

"That's easy enough," the old woman told him, "if you do as I tell you. In the evening, one of the Princesses will bring you some wine. Take care not to drink it, and when she has gone, pretend to be asleep."

Then the old woman gave him a cloak.

"Take this," she said. "As soon as you put it on, you will become invisible, and then you can follow the Princesses wherever they go."

The soldier thanked her and went on his way to the King's palace.

That night he was given a room next to the Princesses' own chamber. Just as he was going to lie down the eldest Princess came to him with a goblet of wine. But the soldier, remembering the words of the old woman, did not drink it, and when the Princess had gone he lay down and began to snore loudly, pretending to be asleep.

When the twelve Princesses heard this they laughed, and immediately they got up and began to dress in all their finery. They skipped and laughed and fidgeted as if they could hardly wait to begin dancing. But the youngest Princess was very quiet, and when the others asked her why, she replied, "I do not know. But I have the strangest feeling that all is not well."

The other Princesses only laughed and called her a simpleton.

"Just listen to him snoring!" they cried. "We have tricked a dozen princes, haven't we? So why should we not trick this old soldier?"

They took a last peep at him as he lay snoring on his bed, and then the eldest Princess went to her bed and clapped her hands. The bed sank into the floor and a trapdoor opened. Down went the twelve Princesses, one by one, with the eldest leading. The soldier leapt up, snatched up the cloak that made him invisible, and followed them.

In his haste he trod on the gown of the youngest Princess when they were halfway down the steps. She started, and cried out to her sisters, "All is not well! Someone caught hold of my gown!"

"Silly creature," called the eldest over her shoulder. "It's nothing but a nail in the wall!"

Down they went, and came out at last into a beautiful grove of trees. The leaves were all of gleaming silver, and the solider, who had never seen such a sight before, reached and broke off a branch from a nearby tree. There was a loud snapping noise, and the youngest Princess cried, "All is not well! Did you hear that noise?" But the eldest replied, "It is only our Princes you hear, shouting for joy because we are coming!"

They came then into a second grove where the leaves were all of gold, and then into a third, where they glittered with diamonds. And in each grove the soldier snapped a branch from a tree, and each time the youngest Princess heard, and cried out in fear. But her sisters only laughed the more.

Soon they came to a great lake. On the water lay twelve little boats with a handsome Prince in each, and how the Princesses laughed and clapped to see them. One of the Princesses stepped into each boat, and when it was the turn of the youngest, the soldier stepped into the boat with her.

"It is hard work rowing tonight," remarked the Prince when they were halfway over the lake. "I am quite worn out."

From the other side of the lake came the sound of music, silvery horns and trumpets, and the soldier saw a magnificent castle with lighted windows. And as soon as they reached the shore the twelve Princesses ran inside and soon were dancing merrily, each with her own Prince.

The soldier himself danced invisibly among them, and amused himself by playing a game. Every time one of the Princesses had a goblet of wine set by her he drank it all up, so that when she put the glass to her mouth, it was empty.

The youngest Princess was very frightened by this, but each time the eldest sister silenced her.

So they danced until cockcrow, until their slippers were quite worn out, and so they *had* to stop. The twelve Princes rowed their partners back across the lake, and this time the soldier went in the boat with the eldest Princess. When they came to the stairs the soldier ran ahead and managed to be back in bed snoring by the time the Princesses stepped back into their own room. They peeped in and saw him there and whispered to each other, "We're quite safe. See – he's fast asleep!"

And they pulled off their tattered slippers, yawning as they did so, and were soon fast asleep themselves.

The soldier could easily have told the secret to the King the very next day, but he wished to see more of this mysterious adventure. So he went again with the Princesses the next night, and again on the third night. But on this last visit, he took away with him a golden cup from the castle, to prove where he had been.

Next morning he was summoned to the King, and he took with him the three branches of silver, gold and diamonds, and the golden cup. The twelve Princesses stood listening at the door, whispering and nudging each other, sure that their secret was safe.

But soon they were staring at each other round-eyed as the soldier began his tale. And when the eldest, who had her eye to the keyhole, saw him take out the three branches and the golden cup and show them to the King, she knew there was no use denying what he said. So the twelve Princesses trooped into the room and confessed the whole story to their father.

"Which of the Princesses will you choose for your wife?" asked the King, when all had been told.

"I am not so young any more," replied the soldier, "so I think I will choose the eldest."

And so they were married, and in time the soldier became king of the whole country, thanks to the old woman in the woods and her good advice.

The Emperor's New Clothes

Once upon a time there lived an Emperor whose greatest delight in life was the wearing and showing off of his rich clothes. It was all he really cared about. If he went to the theatre, or for a drive through the streets, it was only because he wanted everyone to see and admire him. He changed his clothes half a dozen times a day, and often his courtiers, instead of saying "The Emperor's in the Council" would say, "The Emperor's in the Wardrobe."

One day, two travellers came to the court.

"We beg to be allowed to make Your Excellency a new suit of clothes," they said. "We make the most beautiful clothes in the world, and the one we should like to weave for you is a very special one indeed."

"Indeed? Tell me about it," replied the Emperor, preening himself.

"It is beautiful beyond compare," said the weavers. "But that is not all. It can only be seen by those who are clever and wise and well suited to their jobs. Those who are dull or stupid or not fit to do their jobs, can't see a single thing. It's quite invisible to them."

"Invisible?" exclaimed the Emperor.

"Invisible," nodded the two men.

"Now this will be very interesting," thought the Emperor. "For one thing, I shall have another fine new suit of clothes. For another, I shall be able to find out who is clever and who is stupid."

"It will be very expensive," added one of the two men. "Naturally. And we shall require a thousand gold pieces in advance."

The Emperor gave orders that the two men were to be given a loom and all the materials they asked for. They set the loom up in a room in the palace and began to order vast quantities of silks and threads – especially *gold* threads. As soon as these arrived, they stuffed them all into their bags and began to work at the empty looms all day and well into the night.

The Emperor could hardly wait to see his new suit. But every time he thought about it he had a queer sinking feeling inside him, when he remembered that it would be quite invisible to anyone who was stupid or not fitted for his job.

"Not, of course, that it could possibly apply to me," he thought. "Everyone says how clever I am, and of course I am the very man to be Emperor!"

All the same, he kept away from the room where the men were working. On the second day he could contain his curiosity no longer and sent one of his most trusted ministers to see how the work was going.

"He will certainly be able to see the cloth," the Emperor told himself. "A wiser man I have never known."

The old Minister went into the room where the work was going on and stared in amazement at the sight of two men busily working away at what looked like a perfectly empty loom. He rubbed his eyes. Still the loom was empty.

"Dear me," thought the Minister. "Am I really stupid? But whatever happens, I mustn't admit it. I must pretend to see the cloth and admire it, to show the world how wise I am, and how well suited to my job!"

"Well, do you like it?" asked one of the men, stepping back as if to admire his work.

"O gracious, yes!" cried the old man. "Upon my word! I hardly know what to say! What colours, what a design, what a perfectly *ravishing* piece of work!"

"We thought you would like it," said the cunning pair. "Perhaps you'll be good enough to tell his Excellency how well it's going? And while you're at it, we shall also need a few more thousand yards of gold thread, and a couple of sacks of pearls."

"O certainly, yes, certainly!" agreed the Minister. "I shall see to it at once!"

Off he went, quite bewildered, and more than a little sad, because he had always tried to serve the Emperor wisely and well, and now it seemed that he was nothing but a simpleton. But even if he were stupid, there was no point in telling everyone so, and he assured the Emperor that the cloth being woven for his new suit was quite the most exquisite he had ever seen in his whole life.

"Good," thought the Emperor. "My Minister is a wise man."

But still he was not quite ready to face seeing the cloth himself, and next day he sent two courtiers to see how the work was going. By now, everyone in the kingdom had heard of the wonderful cloth that could be seen only by the wise and the clever. The two courtiers came back rather pale, but praising the work highly, and bringing an order for still more gold thread and silks.

At last the day came when the Emperor simply had to go and see for himself. He went into the room, and there were the two men working away for dear life on a loom that had not a single thread or stitch to be seen! The Emperor was horrified.

"I'm a fool!" he thought. "I'm a simpleton! I'm unfit for my job! O dear, O dear!"

But he forced a smile to his lips, because everyone was watching him to see what he would say.

"Ravishing!" he said at last. No one spoke.

"Ravishing!" he said again, more loudly this time, and immediately all the courtiers and officials who were with him began saying to one another, "Ravishing! Wonderful! Miraculous! Out of this world!"

"I shall appoint you Lord High Weavers," said the Emperor, and gave each of the men a medal to pin on his suit.

"Your Excellency must wear a suit made of this cloth for the Grand Procession next week!" said the Chief Courtier, determined not to be outdone in praising the cloth. After all, he told himself, if the *Emperor* could see the cloth, it *must* be there!

"O – should I?" said the Emperor. "You don't think my scarlet silk, with the gold lace cuffs and —"

"No, Your Excellency, with respect," said the Chief Courtier. "This very cloth. You owe it to your people. They have all heard of this wonderful cloth, and can hardly wait to see it. At least," he coughed behind his hand, "the *wise* ones can hardly wait to see it!"

The court laughed merrily and the Emperor himself managed to force out a titter.

Before the Grand Procession the two weavers worked all night with sixteen candles burning. They pretended to take the cloth from the loom, their great scissors clipped at the air, and they stitched busily with empty needles. No one could doubt that they were actually making a suit of clothes.

Then the Emperor arrived with his courtiers. The weavers bowed before him with a great flourish and then held out their arms saying, "Here is the coat, here are the breeches, and this is the cloak! We beg you to try them, for we're sure you'll be delighted. You won't even know you have anything on, because the cloth is so fine that it's light as gossamer!"

The Emperor took off the clothes he was wearing and they pretended to put on him the clothes they had made.

"How does that feel?" they asked, and "It's not too tight is it, Your Excellency?"

"O no, no, I assure you!" cried the Emperor, craning and peering before the glass in the hope that he might catch a glimpse of the suit and prove himself not such a fool after all. "It's the most comfortable suit I have ever worn."

"The fit is wonderful!" sighed the courtiers, shaking their heads. "And as for the colours! And the design! Magnificent!"

Two chamberlains stooped and picked up the invisible train. The Emperor was ready.

Outside the palace the streets were packed with excited people all waiting for the first glimpse of the Emperor's new clothes.

The Emperor stepped out of the palace and felt his skin break out into a rash of goose pimples. There was a short silence, and then a great cheer went up. People leaned out of the windows, crying,

"Hurrah! Hurrah for the Emperor's new clothes!"

"Just look at that coat!"

"What style, what colours, what fit!"

Not a single person there was ready to admit that in fact he could see nothing at all. Every man shouted more loudly than his neighbour, to prove that he could see the clothes and was clever and wise and fitted for his job.

The Emperor himself, deafened by the applause and shouting, was just beginning to rid himself of a strong suspicion that he was walking out stark naked, when a child's voice rang out from the crowd,

"But he's got nothing on!"

There was a hush. The Emperor kept his eyes fixed ahead and felt the goose pimples break out afresh. The voice came again in the silence, clear and high, because it came from a little child who didn't care a fig whether he was thought wise or not.

"He hasn't got anything *on*!" A whispering went through the crowd.

"There's a child here says the Emperor's got nothing on! Not a stitch on, he says!"

The whisper grew louder, it hissed like waves on the shingle,

"Not a stitch on! Nothing on at all!"

Until at last they all shouted out together,

"Why, but he hasn't anything on at all!"

The Emperor groaned inwardly, for he knew they were right. He only needed his goose pimples to tell him that. But he was, after all, the Emperor, so he pretended not to have heard. He drew himself up more proudly than ever and walked on, with the chamberlains stiffly behind him, bearing the train that wasn't even there.

The Princess and the Pea

There was once a Prince who wished to marry a Princess, but she must be a *real* Princess. He travelled the world far and wide in search of her, but though he met many Princesses of every kind, he could never be quite certain in his own heart whether or not she was a *real* Princess. There was always some little fault with each one that seemed to show him that she was not his true bride.

At last, sad at heart, because he really *did* wish to marry, he returned home.

One night soon afterwards there was a terrible storm. The thunder roared and the lightning flashed and the rain came down in sheets and in the midst of it all came a knocking at the palace gates.

The King went to see who was there, and there stood a Princess, looking a very sad sight indeed. Water trickled from her hair and poured from her clothes and her shoes squelched as she stepped inside. But she said that she was a real Princess and that she wished to stay for the night.

"We shall see whether she is a real Princess or not," thought the old Queen, who found it hard to believe that the girl was a Princess at all, with her bedraggled locks and ruined clothes.

She went into the guest chamber and there made up the bed in a special way. First she took all the bedclothes off and laid a single pea on the

bedstead. Then she took twenty mattresses and piled them on top of the pea, and next piled twenty feather beds on top of the mattresses. The Princess was shown to her chamber and climbed up into the bed.

Next morning when she rose the Queen asked her,

"And did you sleep well last night?"

"I hardly slept a wink!" replied the Princess. "I tossed and turned the whole night through. I could feel something hard digging into me, and sure enough, I'm black and blue all over this morning. It was terrible!"

At this, they all saw at once that here, at last, was a real Princess. After all, she had felt a single pea through twenty mattresses and twenty feather beds. Nobody but a real Princess could have so delicate a sense of feeling.

And so the Prince took her gladly as his wife, certain that at last he had found a real Princess. And as for the pea, it was taken and put into a museum, where it may still be seen, if no one has stolen it.

And this, you may depend upon it, is a true story.